Everybody loves a scary story. Now you can enjoy tales that come with a good dose of fright, lots of suspense and a bit of humour too! Phobia books are about all your favourite spooky subjects such as monster aliens, haunted houses, scary dolls and magical powers that go haywire.

Read on if you dare!

PEDIOPHOBIA

THE FEAR OF DOLLS

EVERYONE IS AFRAID OF SOMETHING.

You might be afraid of quite a number of things. But a **PHOBIA** is a very special fear. It is deep and strong and long-lasting. It is hard to explain why people have phobias — sometimes they seem to come out of nowhere.

From the first chapter of this book, when Jas and her family arrive at a weird old hotel and find a room filled with dolls, you'll be hooked! You might feel a strange chilll, even if you're reading on a sunny day. You might feel that somewhere, where you can't see them, dolls are staring at you with their glassy, lidless eyes. . .

1

The north shore of Lake Superior was everything to me.

Maybe that's overstating it. Still, my family spent a long weekend there at the end of every summer. It was one last burst of perfection before school for me and my brother, Jason.

That summer, however, was different.

We drove past the Lakeview Inn, where we usually spent our special week. It sat right on the beach in the middle of town.

This year, though, we couldn't get a room.

Dad tried to book our usual suite, but they said that part of the inn was being renovated. All the other suites were already reserved.

"It looks fine to me," I said as I looked out of the window of Mum's car.

"I'm sure they didn't lie to me, Jas," Dad said, not even looking up from the crossword puzzle on his lap, probably the twentieth one he'd done since we left the house.

Jas was me, of course – short for Jasmine.

"She's right, Dad," Jason said. "I can't see any work being done at all."

"All right, that's enough," Dad said. "I'm sure they're doing work inside. Now let's move on. I'm sure this new place will be just as good."

"Even better," Mum put in as the car sailed right past town. "It's not right in town, so it'll be even more relaxing."

"And there won't be any shops, Wi-Fi, coffee shops, pizza or doughnuts within walking distance," I added.

"Here it is," Mum said. She turned the car off the wide street and onto a gravel road that weaved into the woods.

The car bumped and bounced along. Mum seemed to catch every rut, pothole and massive bump along the trail.

"This can't be right," I said. "Are you sure this isn't some creepy old hunter's driveway?"

Dad had his phone out and was looking through his holiday notes. "The man on the phone said it was really out of the way," he said. "Though he didn't mention off-roading . . ."

"This is how they live up here, kids," Mum said. She clicked the car into four-wheel drive. "I bet this road is closed six months of the year too."

"It ought to be closed all twelve," Jason said.

I laughed.

Mum slowly turned along one more curve. The lake came into view. It glittered in the afternoon sun as though it was made of frosted glass.

"It's so beautiful," I said, in awe.

"Most beautiful sight in the world," Dad said. He turned around and smiled at me. I had to admit it was good to be back, even at the wrong inn.

Even with a name like . . .

"Devil's Mooring," Mum said as she pulled into the gravel car park. "Here we are."

We climbed out. I stood there staring at the inn. It had two storeys, and the front was an ornate A-frame. Or it was ornate at one time. At this moment in time, the paint had peeled and faded, the wood had rotted and some of the letters above the door had worn away.

All I could make out of the old sign was *come to Devil's ring.*

2

Dad handed me my duffel bag. "In we go!" he said, far too cheerfully for the setting.

Jason rolled his eyes at me, and we followed Mum and Dad inside.

The reception was dark and dusty. An old man stood behind the reception desk as if he'd been there forever, watching the door and waiting for us.

"Good afternoon." His voice was as dusty as the reception. His hair – ragged and grey – hung just past his ears. He wore a high collar, like someone from an old painting, and a fancy-looking suit.

"Hi!" Mum called back as we crossed the big reception.

We got closer, and I saw now his sunken cheeks, the frizzled ends of his hair, the tattered cloth of his collar and the creases in his suit.

"I trust you had a pleasant drive?" the old man said.

My dad opened his mouth to reply, but he didn't get the chance.

"Please follow me," the old man said. He came out from behind the reception desk and walked on long, lean legs down the corridor. Though his stride was slow, he covered a lot of distance. Even Jason had to hurry to keep up.

"I was so pleased," he said casually as we hurried alongside him, "to hear a family would be staying with us to close the season."

"Oh?" Mum said. "Are we the only family staying here right now?"

Dad grabbed my hand and gave it a reassuring squeeze.

"I'd have to check the registry, madame," the man replied as he turned a corner.

Ahead, the sconces flickered in the wide, red-carpeted corridor. An intricate pattern of yellow and purple and teal zigzagged along the carpeting.

Down the middle, it was faded from years of being walked on.

"But you said—" Dad started.

"Here we are," the man said, cutting him off. He stopped in front of a door marked *181*.

"Hey, one eight one!" Dad said. "Just like your birthday, honey!"

"Right," I said. "Eighteenth of January. Weird."

"Boooo!" Jason said, waggling his fingers at me.

The innkeeper pulled out a key and opened the door. Then he bowed to welcome us in, dropping the key into Dad's hand as we stepped inside.

"Wow," Jason said. "It's huge."

It was — much bigger than the suite we usually got at the Lakeview. There was a kitchenette just inside the door. The living room sprawled. A fireplace — with a fire already burning – sat nestled in a sunken seating area. Beyond that, a sliding door led out to a private patio.

The three doors – two on one wall, and the third on another – were the bedrooms.

Maybe this place would be better than the Lakeview Inn.

"I'm sure everything will be to your liking," the man said. He was about to leave, and then stopped in the doorway. "I nearly forgot."

He walked right up to me where I stood in the middle of the living room. "Young lady," he said. He grinned, and I had never seen anything so ghastly in all my life. He had all his teeth, but they were too big, too yellow and chipped and cracked like sun-baked bones in Death Valley.

"I was especially pleased to learn *you'd* be staying here," he went on.

I took two steps back and stumbled into the sunken seating area. Jason caught me by the shoulders.

"M-me?" I said.

"Come with me," he said, and gestured with one long, crooked finger to follow him.

I glanced at Jason, and he took the hint and went with me to follow the old man into one of the bedrooms.

"It's the perfect bedroom for you, don't you think?" the man said, standing in the open doorway.

I stepped inside with Jason's hand in mine and gasped.

My room was lined with shelves, three high on three walls, and the shelves were full of staring, glass-eyed dolls.

My breath caught in my throat. I held tightly to Jason's arm to stop myself from falling over.

The man smiled at me, his face stretching into a monstrous grin. "I knew you'd like it," he said in a raspy whisper.

"If she likes any of them," he added, speaking to our parents, "they're for sale, prices as marked!"

Leaving me and Jason in the bedroom, he stepped past us, taking one of my hands in his. He patted it gently. "I'm so pleased to have a little girl staying here," he said. "A guest who might appreciate our little collection."

Little girl? I thought angrily. *I'm thirteen!*

3

"I think you got the biggest room," Jason said. "Lucky." He left me alone sitting on the double bed with fifty dolls staring at me.

"I don't feel very lucky," I muttered when he was out of earshot.

I should probably explain. You see, my brother didn't know – and neither did my parents – but I was terrified of dolls.

Maybe I didn't even know yet, not really.

Because I'd played with fashion dolls as a kid, and with princesses from my favourite films. But the dolls in this room at Devil's Mooring scared me to pieces. These were the kind that seemed older than my grandparents. They wore realistic clothes, like a baby might have worn two hundred years ago.

Their painted lips curved in slight smiles. It made them look mean.

Their round cheeks glowed pale pink, so they looked almost alive.

And their eyes. Their glass eyes shined, reflecting the light from the fixture over the bed. The light flickered as the ceiling fan turned slowly.

As the light flickered, their eyes seemed to shift in their heads.

I jumped up from the bed and ran from the room.

"What's your problem?" Jason said as I nearly knocked him down.

"Swap rooms with me," I said, nodding back towards the doll room.

"No way," Jason said. "It's way too girly for me. You heard the innkeeper."

"Don't be ridiculous," I said. "That's such an outdated way to think."

"It doesn't matter anyway," Jason said, walking away. "I've already mostly unpacked in *my* room. And my room has a TV."

"What?" I said, almost forgetting the creepy dolls. "Jason gets a TV?"

Mum rolled her eyes.

"A TV that gets one channel," Dad said with a playful smile. "The local channel from town."

"I'm sure Jason will enjoy watching the panel of locals discussing the migratory fish of Lake Superior," Mum joked.

Jason took a moment to glare at the rest of us before retreating into his room and closing the door.

"What about you two?" I said. "Do you want to swap rooms with me?"

"What?" Mum said. "Why would we do that? Ours has a bathroom."

"And we've already unpacked," Dad added.

"But—," I started to say, but I couldn't bring myself to admit I was afraid of the dolls.

Instead I said, "The dolls are so childish."

"Honey," Mum said, putting a hand on my cheek, "*you* are a child. I think the doll room is sweet. And if you want to pick out your favourite, maybe one will make a nice souvenir for you!"

"Ugh," I said, pulling away. I went into the doll room and closed the door.

I lay on the bed and stared at the ceiling fan, forcing myself not to even glance at the glassy-eyed little creeps surrounding me.

Before long, the fan's lazy spin lulled me to drowsiness. I rolled onto my side, thinking I might have a quick nap before dinner.

But on my side, all I could see were shelves of dolls. This one, with dark and curly hair tied in red ribbons. That one, with straight white hair, as fine as spun sugar.

Another, a boy — his hair brown and sticking out in shaggy locks from beneath a blue cap.

And the one that moved: a girl in a green dress with puffs at the shoulders. She had eyes to match her dress and a thousand dark freckles. Her strawberry hair was frizzy and needed a comb.

That girl climbed down from her shelf and crossed the wooden floor, but I couldn't move. I could only watch.

She scaled the big bed, a little doll mountain climber, and she wrapped her tiny wooden hands around my throat.

She began to squeeze. Her glassy eyes flickered. Her sinister smile stretched. I could not breathe. I could not throw her off. I could only stare into her unloving eyes and hear the childish laughter of every doll in the room.

"Wake up, Jas!"

My eyes sprang open. I stared up at the lazily spinning ceiling fan, still on my back.

So I'd fallen asleep.

"What?" I said. Jason stood beside the bed.

"I said wake up," he said. "It's time to go to dinner."

4

At Tom and Bob's Pizza in town, I sat in the
corner of the booth and stared out of the restaurant's
front windows.

It was a cloudy afternoon. The overcast sky
reflected in the great lake so everything from the
rocky beach to the horizon and beyond was slate
grey and sad looking.

I hardly touched my pizza.

"We probably won't come here again this trip,
Jas," Mum said, leaning across the table. "You look
forward to Tom and Bob's every year."

I picked up a slice of pizza and took a little bite. It was already cold. The sausage seemed bland, the cheese rubbery.

"I'm not very hungry," I said.

Jason immediately reached over from next to me and snagged one of my slices.

"You can finish it," I said. "I don't care."

Jason looked at me, eyes wide, for a moment. Then he shrugged and grabbed three more slices.

When Jason had stuffed himself completely, we headed down to the walkway along the beach. He and Dad started skimming rocks. Mum perched on a boulder and enjoyed the good mobile reception in town, as we'd had none at the inn.

I decided to take a walk on my own.

"Don't go too far!" Mum called after me.

I was almost at the walkway out to the lighthouse when I came upon a boy about my age. He was crouched on the beach building a tower of small, flattish stones. That was a thing visitors liked to do on the lake shore. A sort of a tradition.

I stopped nearby and watched him add stones to the tower. He was very careful. After a few minutes and a few stones, he sat back and said, "Hi."

"Hi," I said. Behind him and west of town, the clouds were breaking up a little. I could see the sunset.

"Are you staying at the Lakeview too?" he asked.

I shook my head. "They didn't have room for us," I said. "We're staying at a place called Devil's Mooring up the shore a bit."

"I've never heard of it," he said, going back to selecting flat rocks for his tower.

I turned to face the lake and squinted into the distance. "You can just see it from here," I said, pointing to a little speck of rusty red near the water, far away.

The boy came up beside me and tried to follow my finger.

"I can't see it at all," he said. Then he turned to

the walkway and called to the old woman sitting on a bench nearby. "Great-gran, do you know the place Devil's Mooring?"

The woman got up from her bench and walked carefully over the rocky ground to stand with us. "Devil's what?" she asked. "Who's your friend?"

"I'm Jasmine," I said, putting out my hand to shake.

She took my hand and patted it gently, looking into my eyes sincerely. "Aren't you a doll," she said.

"Devil's *Mooring*," the boy repeated.

His great-grandmother stared thoughtfully over the lake. "I *do* remember that place," she finally said.

"Great-gran lived here for years," the boy explained. "She moved down to the city when it got too much for her to drive down to visit all the time."

"I think it closed down in the 1960s," the old woman went on.

"Oh, no," I said. "We're staying there. It's definitely still open."

But the boy's great-grandmother didn't seem to hear me. "The owner of that place, or maybe it was his wife," she went on as she strolled slowly towards the gentle surf, "hand made the most lovely dolls. I think I bought one as a very little girl."

"They still have them," I said.

"Such beautiful dolls," the old woman said, her voice faraway and somehow both sad and happy at once.

"We'd better get back to the inn, Great-gran," the boy said as he took her by one arm.

Without another word, the boy and the old woman walked off towards the Lakeview.

5

Back at the Devil's Mooring Inn, Mum and Dad settled on the sofa to watch a film. I ushered Jason into his room and closed the door.

"What are you doing?" he said, annoyed.

"Have you noticed anything weird about this place?" I asked, sitting on the edge of the bed.

Jason dropped to the floor to do his push-ups. He did like fifty every night.

"Weird?" he said between puffed breaths. "Besides the dude who runs the place?"

"No, him too," I said.

"And the name?" Jason said, doing another push-up. "And the fact that clearly no one else is staying here even though it's like the biggest weekend of the summer for trips up north?"

"Yeah, all that," I said.

"Nah, nothing weird about that," Jason said. He rolled onto his side. "What are you getting at, anyway? So it's a weird place. So what?"

"So I met this boy in town after dinner," I started.

Of course, Jason couldn't let that go. "Ooh," he said, and he made a load of kissy sounds. "Shall we tell Mum to start planning the wedding?"

"Shut up," I said. "The point is his great-grandmother was with him. She seemed to think this inn had closed like fifty or sixty years ago."

"So some old lady has a bad memory," he said. "Quick, hand me my phone. I have to send a text to the FBI's supernatural division."

"You're so annoying," I said. I got up to leave.

"Takes one to know one!" he called after me.

I slammed his door and dropped onto the sofa between Mum and Dad.

When the film ended and the credits were scrolling up the screen, Mum yawned. "Time for you to get to bed," she said.

"I'm not tired," I said. The truth was I didn't want to go to bed in that awful bedroom with those awful dolls.

"Well," Dad said, "we are on holiday. And that love story she likes so much is coming on next. With that new actor."

"Let's watch that," I said. I cuddled against my dad.

"Fine, fine," Mum said. "But there will be no sleeping in tomorrow. I want to get some doughnuts *and* hit the hiking trail nice and early."

"OK, Mum," I said as the film started. "No problem."

I *was* tired, and before long, I fell asleep.

I was hardly aware of Dad carrying me to bed. But when I woke up, cherubic faces watched me

from the shelves. Their glass eyes shined in the pink morning light coming through the windows.

I sat up. Outside, just steps from my window, the innkeeper stood facing the sunrise. In one hand he held a heavy-looking cloth bag.

When he turned around and saw me, I lay back down and covered myself with the blanket.

Knock-knock. "Rise and shine, Jas," Dad called through the door. "Doughnuts wait for no man – nor girl."

I peeked out from under the blanket. The innkeeper was no longer at the window.

I dressed quickly. Before hurrying to join my family, I stopped to look at the dolls. I don't know what came over me, but almost without thinking I knocked every single one of them onto the floor into a pile.

Then I grabbed the blanket from my bed and raised it high, like a pretend parachute. It fluttered and fell slowly over the piles of little wooden boys and girls.

Just before it covered them in darkness and hid them completely, one of them — she had blonde hair in tight curls, a single fat blue ribbon holding back her ringlets — looked at me and sneered.

6

The morning was beautiful. The queue for doughnuts was long, but no one minded. The sun was out, and a cool breeze blew in off the lake to ensure it didn't get too hot.

When Mum drove into the state park at the bottom of the hiking trail, a few fluffy-looking clouds had made their way overhead.

"Nice day for a hike," said the woman at the gate as we paid for admittance. "Might rain later."

I looked up at the beautiful summer sky. It certainly didn't look like rain.

"You know what they say about weather at the lake," the woman at the gate said, fixing her crooked eyes on me. "If you don't like the weather, wait half an hour."

Mum parked the car. Dad put our doughnuts in his pack, and we started to hike.

We were halfway up the trail when Dad stopped at an overlook. "I think the attendant might have been right," he said.

I stepped up next to him and leaned on the railing. It shook a little, as if it might break.

I could see the town from there and the lake beyond. The clouds over the horizon were grey and heavy-looking.

"Is it a storm?" I asked.

"Looks like it," Dad said. "Pretty far off, though. I think we'll have plenty of time to finish our hike."

But the woman at the gate must have known more about Great Lakes weather than Dad. Fifteen minutes later, with still a long way to go on the hike, the grey clouds had caught up with us.

The storm sat just off the hillside and seemed to weigh down the sky. I felt I had to duck, as if I might bang my head on the clouds.

I felt the first drop on my cheek. It was big and fat and exploded on my face. "Dad," I said, but a moment later, the skies opened.

"Dad!" I screamed.

"Hurry, hurry!" Mum shouted, pulling her light jacket over her head. She moved quickly up the trail.

Dad ushered me and Jason ahead of him.

I struggled to keep up with Mum. Jason shoved me from behind, hurrying me along.

Quickly the trail was wet – too wet for safe footing. I used the slim trees along the trail like a sideways ladder, but it was no good. My feet slid, and I had to half-crawl and half run.

Jason pushed past me. Dad took my arm and helped me along. Still, we both stumbled and slipped. Before long, we were soaking wet and muddy up to our waists.

We were near the peak. A small log building sat off the trail among the trees. "There!" I shouted over the din of the storm.

Thunder clapped. Dad nodded and whistled with his fingers between his lips.

Jason and Mum turned, and I pointed urgently ahead.

We slipped and tripped up the hill, but we made it. Up close now, I saw the building was older than I'd realized. It was overgrown with crawling vines. Young trees sprouted from its foundation. Clearly no one had done any work here in years.

Jason banged the door open with his shoulder and we all followed him inside. Something scurried. Or several things scurried. Mice, squirrels – who knows.

It was dark and musty. An old aluminium table sat in the corner, covered with dust. Against the far wall was a plain-looking desk. An old black phone sat on it, along with a stack of papers weighed down with a rock.

There was also some old-looking electrical stuff.

"A CB radio," Dad said. He picked up the mouthpiece and clicked the button. Nothing happened. "Wow, this stuff must have been untouched for decades."

He blew on the mouthpiece, and dust puffed into the air. He coughed and coughed.

There was a door behind the desk. I checked the knob. It was locked.

"Storage room, probably," Dad said.

I picked up the old phone and put it to my ear. "I think it's dead," I said, replacing the receiver. I wiped the thick dust on my leggings.

Mum wiped off the seat of a faded green vinyl sofa. "Well," she said, sitting down with a groan, "if it's been abandoned for fifty years, we can still wait out the storm here, right?"

"Of course," Jason said. He sat next to Mum.

I flipped through the stack of papers on the desk. They were forms of some kind. Each had blank boxes for names and addresses. At the bottom, they asked for credit card information.

In the middle, a larger box asked for "style" and "quantity".

"That's weird," I said aloud.

"What is, honey?" Dad said. He came up next to me and put an arm around my shoulders.

"Well, it looks like whoever stayed in this cabin," I said, "was selling something."

"Huh, that's odd," Dad said. "I just thought–"

"Doughnuts time!" Jason interrupted as he pulled Dad's pack right off his back.

Then the locked door to the storage room flew open.

I screamed.

7

"Whoa, whoa!" said the middle-aged woman who stepped through the door. "Didn't mean to scare you, doll."

She wore a tan and green uniform and a wide-brimmed hat. A park ranger.

"You just startled us that's all," Dad said, forcing a smile. But he was holding me close, and I could hear his heart racing.

"We thought the place was abandoned," Mum said, rising from the sofa. She wiped her wet hair off her forehead.

"I hope we're not intruding," Dad added. "Just getting shelter from the storm."

"Oh, of course not," the woman said. "I'm here the whole season. It's nice to have visitors."

"All summer?" I asked. "But . . ."

"Yes?" she said, leaning towards me. She smiled at me, and it seemed eerily familiar. Closer now, I could see that she wore a lot of make-up to hide wrinkles and freckles. Her hair was also dyed to hide the grey. The roots were unmistakable.

"It's just that it's so dusty," I said.

"Jasmine!" Mum snapped. "That is very rude."

The woman laughed. "Oh, I don't mind one bit," she said. She put a hand on my shoulder. It felt cold. "When you live alone and don't get any visitors, I suppose you let a few things go."

"Do you know Devil's Mooring?" I blurted out. I didn't mean to. I just suddenly had to ask.

"The inn?" the park ranger said. "Of course. The owners are friends of mine. Whenever I get down from this mountain, I always stop by for lunch or dinner. Sometimes even a night in one of their rooms with a view of the lake."

I felt relieved. The conversation with that boy and his great-grandmother had me thinking our inn was in some other dimension, an upside-down world with evil dolls. At least the park ranger had heard of it.

Still, the relief didn't last. The nagging worry in my chest faded only for a moment. Then, looking into the park ranger's deep-set eyes, it came back ten-fold.

"Is there a toilet I can use?" I asked.

"Sure," the woman said. She pulled open the door she'd come out of. "It's just through here."

I looked in. Beyond the doorway it was pitch dark. If there was a door to the toilet on the far side of the room, I certainly couldn't see it.

"Thanks," I said, stepping slowly and blindly into the room. I reached out my hands in front of me as I went, hoping not to knock anything over.

But my foot caught the edge of a table, and I went sprawling. So did the table. We landed with a crash, and the light flicked on.

The park ranger and my dad stood in the doorway behind me. I lay in the middle of the room, a tall pedestal table on the floor beside me.

I pushed myself up and turned my head. On my other side lay something that had fallen off the table: a doll.

I jumped to my feet and spun. The small living room was lined with shelves just like back at the inn, and the shelves were full of dolls.

A boy there, in a sailor suit. There, a girl, her skin dark and her eyes bright. Beside her, slightly larger, a joyful-looking man with a moustache that twirled from his lips. And next to him, a woman in a fine-looking green dress, her hair set in curls on her head and her hands set primly in her lap.

There were freckles, glasses, beards, handbags, winter coats and summer suits, swimming trunks and a set of tiny skis and poles.

I burst from the back room, shoved past the park ranger and my dad, and ran from the old building and into the woods.

8

The rain had all but stopped, but the ground was wet. Fallen leaves and rotten wood and sprouting mushrooms made the ground impossibly slippery, but I couldn't stop.

I slid my way between trees, unable to find the actual path. It was dangerous. It was stupid. But I didn't care. I would risk my life to get as far away from those dolls – and from that woman – as I could, as quickly as I could.

I stumbled along, slowing my descent by getting my hands on as many narrow trees as I could as I went.

My leggings tore. My socks were drenched inside my boots. As the hillside grew steeper, I couldn't slow myself. My legs seemed to fly on their own.

In front of me was wide-open space. I was about to launch off the mountain.

I slammed into the railing at the overlook, the same place I'd stood with my dad less than an hour ago. The railing bent and snapped.

The railing dangled, barely attached to its cement footing above me. I dangled over the abyss. I couldn't look down.

With one hand, I held tight to the metal bar. With the other, I struggled to reach up to grab hold of the cement and pull myself to safety.

But as I reached, the metal railing screeched in protest and snapped.

I fell. My hands swung wildly, grabbing for any hold. I snapped branches. I knocked against a tree trunk as my feet scrambled on the steep ground, unable to find a perch.

I tumbled and rolled and slammed into a fat old tree stump. I would have fallen further if I hadn't wrapped my arms around it in a desperate hug.

"Jasmine!" Mum screamed from high above me. "Jasmine, please answer!"

"I'm OK!" I said, my voice wet and too quiet.

"I think I'm OK!" I added, a little louder.

"Stay there," Dad called down to me. "We're coming for you."

"No, I'm OK!" I shouted back.

It was mostly true. I'd definitely have bruises. And my legs were bleeding a little where my leggings had ripped. But I could walk. I got my footing and made my way back to the trail. It was flatter there, and even beginning to dry.

I knew my family was hurrying down to reach me, but I didn't wait. I jogged the rest of the way to the car and leaned on the door.

It was familiar and clean. I laid my forehead on the backseat window and closed my eyes to catch my breath and try to calm down.

"Jasmine!" Dad shouted.

I didn't lift my head till he was at the car with his arms around me. I turned around then and found I was crying.

Back at the inn, I dragged my feet across reception.

"My goodness," the old innkeeper said. "What happened to you folks?"

I didn't answer.

"Just got caught in some rain," Dad said. I could hear the fake smile in his voice.

Mum unlocked our suite. I sleepily made my way to my room, pleased I'd find the shelves empty and those wicked creations in a heap under a blanket.

But that's not what I found at all. All the dolls were back in their places. The blonde-haired girl with perfect ringlets and a blue ribbon sat in the centre of the shelf on the far wall.

"Nice try," she said.

I screamed and ran from the room.

When Mum grabbed me as I ran through the living room, I screamed and tried to get away. Maybe it was her eyes. They're dark brown, and I think for an instant they seemed like glass, like a doll's eyes.

I saw my reflection in Mum's eyes, wide with fear for my safety, and in the reflection, even I looked wrong – like a doll, made of wood, with round cheeks tinted pink.

She led me to the sofa and laid me down. Dad put a pillow under my head.

"I'm sorry," I said, barely a whisper. It was all I had strength for. "I should have told you I was terrified in there."

"In where, dear?" Mum said.

I looked towards my bedroom. "The dolls," I said. "They hate me. I mean, I hate them."

Dad sat on the coffee table. Mum went to the phone and called the reception desk.

"No one's picking up," Mum said. "This place."

"All right, let's all try to calm down," Dad said. "I'm sure they can put us in a different suite. If not, certainly Jason won't mind swapping rooms for the next couple of nights."

"What?!" Jason said. "No way. I—"

Dad and Mum glared at him.

"Fine, fine," Jason said. "Anything for my crazy little sister, right?"

He slapped my foot and winked at me.

There came a knock at the door.

"Everything all right in there?" the innkeeper said from the corridor.

"Good," Mum said, rising from the sofa beside me. "I'll get us a new suite right now."

Mum opened the door, and the old man came in. He spotted me at once and limped towards me. "Is she ill?" he asked. He didn't look worried. Not exactly. Instead he looked . . . disappointed.

"She'll be fine," Mum said. "But we would really like to be moved to a different suite."

"Can't be done," the innkeeper said before Mum could even explain. "No vacancies. We're full up."

"Full up?" Jason said. "Is he joking?"

The old man sneered at Jason and fixed him with a glare.

"We haven't seen another soul in the inn since we've been here," Dad said. "Not in reception, not on the beach, not in the car park."

"Oh, plenty of souls here," the innkeeper said. He chuckled at his own joke, if that's what it had been.

He gave me another long and curious look before turning to leave. "Oh, I nearly forgot why I came down here," he said in the doorway as he turned around. "The dolls in your room, little girl."

My heart thumped. "What about them?"
I asked.

"My wife was cleaning while you folks were on your hike," he said. "She found all the dolls in a heap on the floor."

"Oh," I said, now truly relieved.

"Mustn't do that again," he added, his voice stern and his chin high in authority. "They're not for playing with unless you plan to buy 'em."

"Sorry," I said. "I won't do that again."

He nodded, turned and left, closing the door behind him.

10

We had a quiet afternoon. Jason got all my stuff out of the doll room and brought it into his room.

"Thanks, Jace," I said from the sofa, smiling up at him. He could be a real monster sometimes, but he was often so sweet. A real doll.

"No problem," he said as he hopped over the arm of the sofa and sat by my feet. "Anything on TV?"

"You don't have to spend time with me just because I'm bonkers," I said. "Go! Enjoy the lake!"

But Jason ignored me. When Mum and Dad went into town to buy some food for dinner on the patio, he and I just sat in front of the TV for a couple of hours.

Jason let me doze. When I woke up, he made me some tea. When sport came on and I groaned, he put on a drama series on a different channel for me.

It was so strange. My parents and my brother now knew how I felt about those dolls. But they hadn't laughed at me. Even Jason was being amazing.

I was sure the rest of the holiday would be great, once I got some rest after the morning's adventure.

"Who wants a burger?" Dad said happily as he and Mum came into the suite, laden with paper bags. "I got burgers, hot dogs, bacon, cheese slices, crisps, dips–"

"We bought half the shop," Mum said, cutting him off with a sly smile. "And fear not: we've plenty of ice cream for pudding."

"Strawberry?" I said, sitting up a bit.

Mum held up the pink tub. "Do I know my little girl?" she said.

"Thanks, Mum," I said. Everyone was being amazing.

Dad and Jason went out on the patio to start up the barbecue. Mum sat in the armchair next to the sofa and read a magazine.

I fell asleep.

When I woke, it was dark in the living room. Mum wasn't in the armchair with her magazine. I had that unsettling feeling of having napped until evening, and for a moment I didn't know where I was, or what time of day it was. But I could smell burgers through the screen door to the patio.

The TV was still on, showing a crime programme from twenty years ago. Two men in overcoats asked a third man in a hoodie where he was on the night of the fifteenth.

The TV turned off with a strange sucking sound. It was quiet. Even the fridge stopped humming.

Power cut, I thought. I sat up. "Mum?" I called. No one answered.

I stood up. My legs were a bit wobbly – maybe from lying around all afternoon, or maybe from my express trip down the cliffside.

"Dad? Jace?" I said through the screen door. But outside it was even darker. I could hear the lake, though, sloshing onto the rocks of the beach. It was a beautiful sound.

It would soon grow to be interminable.

"Maybe everyone's gone to bed already," I muttered to myself. "Maybe I slept through dinner."

I pulled the sliding door closed, quieting the lake a bit. The lulling *whoosh* still found its way inside through the open windows.

A single light glowed under the door to my bedroom. Jason's bedroom now, of course.

But if there's a power cut, I thought, *why is there a light on in there?*

"A book light," I whispered to myself. "Jason probably brought one from home, battery operated."

I knocked gently on the door, hoping to see my brother's comforting face in a moment. But he didn't answer.

I turned the knob quietly and opened the door. The bed was empty. The light came from the fixture, where the fan spun lazily.

"There she is," said the blonde girl with the ringlets and the blue ribbon. "We've waited all afternoon, you know."

"Jason!" I screamed. "Mum! Dad! Where are you?!"

I turned from the doll room and ran for the door to the suite. I grabbed the doorknob and tugged at it madly. The door was locked.

I turned the deadbolt. I flicked the little lock set into the knob. The door would not budge.

The patio, I thought, and I started across the living room. But before I passed the door to the doll room, it opened again. Light poured into the living room, and with it a horde of those fiendish, tiny boys and girls.

"There's nothing to be afraid of, Jasmine," said one of the dolls. He was tall, and looked a bit stronger than the others. He had a wry smile. I almost found his face comforting.

"Jason?" I said.

I ran to the kitchen and grabbed a broom. As the dolls moved closer, I swung it wildly, knocking a few against the wall. One little wooden arm knocked loose. Another lost her red ribbon.

"Jasmine, darling," said my mother's voice. I found her face – big brown eyes, tiny nose set between high, proud cheekbones. "Stop this at once. You're making a scene."

I'm not ashamed to say I screamed then, the loudest I'd ever screamed in my life. But it did no good. I dropped the broom, and the horde of dolls overcame me.

I fell. My head banged hard on the tile floor of the kitchenette, and everything went black.

✦

It's not bad now. It's quiet here, and sometimes I'm facing a window so I can look at the lake. I'm with my family too. Dad's painted-on beard isn't quite right. Mum's glasses have strange frames and no lenses. I suppose she can't see very well. Jason's dressed in really old-fashioned clothes. He looks funny, and I imagine the two of us laughing about it one day.

We can't laugh though, of course. Our mouths don't work at all.

I just hope when I'm bought – *if* I'm bought – that the buyers take the rest of my family too. I'd hate to sit on a shelf somewhere all alone.

GLOSSARY

aluminium type of metal

authority official, or coming from someone who has the power to give orders

dimension different world from our own

drowsiness nearly asleep

flickered burned unsteadily or with a constantly changing light

horde large and unorganized group of individuals

innkeeper owner or manager of an inn

interminable seemingly endless

kitchenette very small kitchen area

rubbery like rubber in appearance or stretchiness

sconce candle holder attached to a wall

sun-baked dried out, chapped or cracked by the sun's heat

vacancies empty or available rooms at a hotel

zigzag move in short, sharp turns or angles from one side to the other

FACE YOUR FEAR!

Now that you've read the story, it's no longer only inside this book. It's also in your brain. Can your brain help you answer the questions below?

1. Think about a scary toy you've seen. Did it seem as haunted as the dolls Jasmine found?

2. Imagine a different ending to the story, where Jasmine and her family escape the hotel. How do they get away from the innkeeper?

3. What hints were there that something was wrong with the Devil's Mooring hotel? Use examples from the text to discuss the scary signs.

4. Can you explain why the innkeeper is so happy that Jasmine is staying at his hotel? What details in the text support your explanation?

5. Jasmine describes the great-grandmother's voice as "Both sad and happy at once" when she's talking about the dolls. What do you think Jasmine means by this?

FEAR FACTORS

pediophobia — the fear of dolls

Scientists believe that a fear of dolls comes from the "uncanny effect" on the brain. "Uncanny" means "oddly different" or "strangely uncomfortable". At first glance, our brains tell us that dolls are humans. Then the brain realizes something is not quite right. The dolls are not human because they're too small. This jumping back and forth in our brains between real and unreal causes the uncanny effect and can produce uneasiness or fear.

In Thailand, a strange fad is collecting human-size dolls. The elaborately dressed dolls are considered good luck charms. But some people believe that the spirits of young children inhabit the human-like toys.

Voodoo dolls have been a part of folklore from Africa to Europe throughout the centuries. The doll is made to resemble a specific living person. Pins are stuck into the doll, with the superstitious wish that the person it looks like will feel pain in those same parts of the body. These dolls, sometimes called poppets, could be made of clay, sticks, rags, wax, paper or carved from tree roots.

The town of Nagoro, Japan, is filled with human-size dolls. There are whole classrooms where seats are filled with only doll pupils. Doll teachers stand in the dark corridors. Doll workers plant and weed nearby fields. Dolls climb trees, sit on front porches and welcome visitors to their village. In 2003, resident Ayano Tsukimi watched as her town's population grew smaller with people dying or leaving for bigger cities. So Ayano started making life-size replicas of the departed, placing them in locations and poses in memory of the real people. Do not visit this town after dark!

ABOUT THE AUTHOR

Steve Brezenoff is the author of more than fifty chapter books for young readers, including the Field Trip Mysteries series, the Ravens Pass series of thrillers and the Return to the Titanic series. He's also written three young-adult novels, *Guy in Real Life*, *Brooklyn, Burning* and *The Absolute Value of -1*. In his spare time, he enjoys playing video games, cycling and cooking. Steve lives in Minnesota, USA, with his wife, Beth, and their son and daughter.

ABOUT THE ILLUSTRATOR

Mariano Epelbaum is a character designer, illustrator and traditional 2D animator. He has been working as a professional artist since 1996, and enjoys trying different art styles and techniques. Throughout his career Mariano has created characters and designs for a wide range of films, TV series, adverts and publications in his native country of Argentina. He has contributed to several books for children, including Fairy Tale Mix-ups, You Choose: Fractured Fairy Tales and Snoops, Inc.

GRIMM
AND
GROSS

only from Raintree